Another Sommer-Time Story

No One Will Ever Know

By Carl Sommer
Illustrated by Dick Westbrook

Advance • HOUSTON
PUBLISHING, INC

Permissions
Advance Publishing, Inc.
6950 Fulton St.
Houston, TX 77022

http://www.advancepublishing.com

First Edition
Printed in Singapore

Library of Congress Cataloging-in-Publication Data

Sommer, Carl, 1930-
    No one will ever know / by Carl Sommer ; illustrated by Dick Westbrook. – 1st ed.
        p.   cm. – (Another Sommer-time story)
    Summary: When four young squirrels ignore the rules and sneak away to Mr. Smith's farm to eat acorns, trouble strikes in the form of a hungry wolf.
    ISBN 1-57537-006-9 (hc : alk. paper). – ISBN 1-57537-052-2 (lib. bdg. : alk. paper)
    [1. Squirrels–Fiction. 2. Wolves–Fiction. 3. Conduct of life–Fiction.] I. Westbrook, Dick, ill. II. Title. III. Series: Sommer, Carl, 1930-   Another Sommer-time story.
PZ7.S696235Np 1997
[E]–dc20   96-24344
                                                          CIP
                                                          AC

No One Will Ever Know

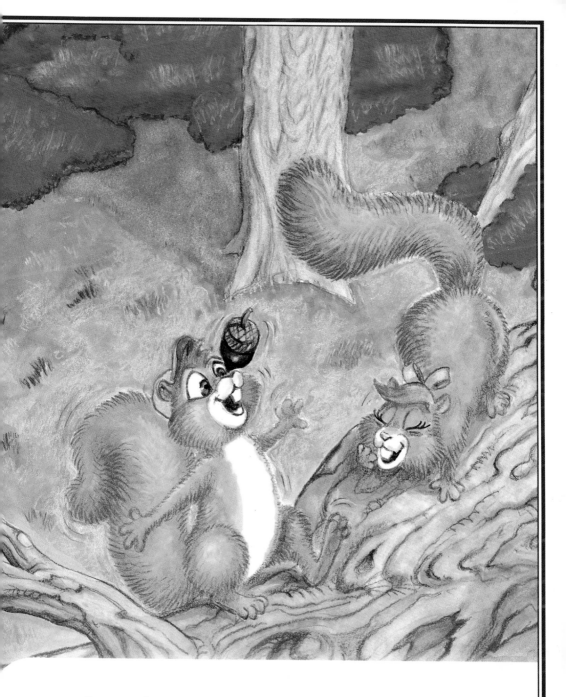

Once there were two happy little squirrels named Johnny and Janie.

They lived with their dad and mom inside a large tree at the edge of a beautiful forest.

Their friends Teddy and Tammy often came to visit. How they loved to play their favorite game, tree tag.

Up and down the trees they raced, jumping across the branches.

All the squirrels were very fast, but no one could catch Johnny—he was the fastest!

One day some older squirrels stopped by.

"Why do you kids stay here eating those small acorns?" yapped the big squirrels rather roughly. "We know a special place that has the biggest and most delicious acorns you have ever tasted."

Then one of them pulled out a giant acorn.

"Wow!" said the young squirrels. Acorns were their favorite food!

"Whew-wee!" Johnny yelled. "That's the biggest acorn I've ever seen! Where did you find it?"

"Across the meadow and over the fence on Mr. Smith's farm," answered the oldest squirrel.

Johnny moaned. "We can't go there."

"Why not?" asked the big squirrels. "No one will ever know."

Janie spoke up. "Dad and Mom say it's dangerous. They say a big, bad wolf might get us."

"Go ahead!" teased the older squirrels. "Stay in your little yard and eat your tiny acorns."

They rubbed their tummies and laughed, "We'll be at Mr. Smith's farm eating those big, delicious acorns!"

With a bounce they hurried off.

Johnny wanted to be like the older squirrels. He spun his cap around and said to Janie, "Why don't we go there just once?"

"And disobey Dad and Mom?" Janie asked. "That's not right!"

"If we don't tell anyone," Johnny argued, "no one will ever know!"

Teddy and Tammy liked Johnny's idea.

"We could go late at night after our parents go to sleep," said Tammy.

"Yeah!" shouted Teddy. "But let's wait until there's a full moon so we can see better."

"But what about that b-i-g . . . b-a-d . . . w-o-l-f?" asked Janie. "He scares me!"

"We'll be real quiet," said Johnny. "I'm sure the wolf will be sleeping."

Finally they all agreed. They could not wait until they could eat those big, delicious acorns.

At last it came—the night of a bright, full moon. Johnny and Janie ate very little for supper that evening.

"Why aren't you eating?" asked Mom.

"Uh, well...we're not hungry," Johnny lied.

He and Janie did not want to eat too much. Tonight they were going to fill their tummies with big, delicious acorns.

After the meal, Johnny and Janie played in the yard. When Mom called out, "Bedtime!" they quickly went inside and climbed into bed.

"That's strange," Dad said to Mom. "They always want to stay up longer. But tonight they went to bed right away."

"Maybe," said Mom, "they are learning that it is best for them to obey."

Soon the house became very quiet. Dad and Mom were sound asleep. But not Johnny and Janie. They were too excited!

It seemed like forever, but finally Janie heard a whistle.

Janie whispered, "Psst! Johnny! I think I hear them."

They jumped out of bed and ran to the window. There stood Teddy and Tammy, waving to them in the bright moonlight.

Very quietly they climbed out the window.

"Shhh!" whispered Johnny. "We don't want to wake up Dad or Mom."

"Okay!" said Janie very softly.

Without a sound they eased down the tree and climbed over the fence to meet Teddy and Tammy.

Everyone had waited so long for this night. Finally they were happily on their way.

The young squirrels laughed and talked about how much fun they were going to have eating those big, delicious acorns. They were especially glad for the two older squirrels who had told them about Mr. Smith's farm.

Suddenly Janie froze. She saw something through the trees!

"Stop!" she cried. "Someone is watching us!"

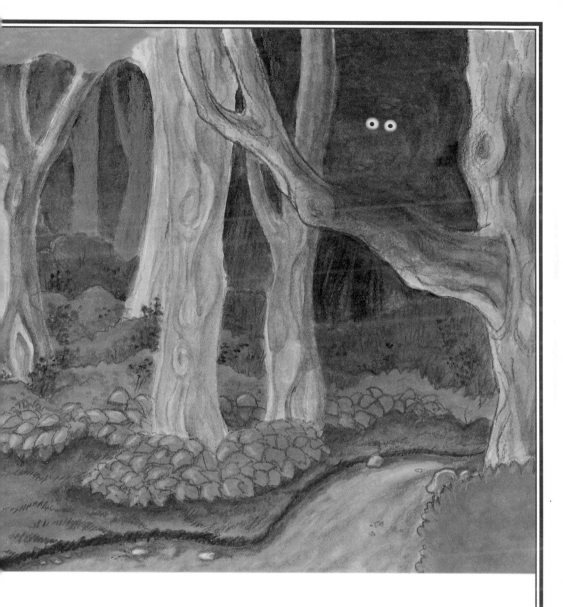

Janie was so afraid she began to shake.

"Wh...wh...where?" asked Johnny.

"Over there!" whispered Janie as she pointed at two beady eyes glowing in the dark. Now they all were scared and shaking.

"Let's go back," begged Tammy.

Then Johnny and Teddy saw the eyes move. They knew who it was!

"Don't be afraid," laughed Johnny.

Teddy giggled. "That's just an old owl."

They tiptoed under the tree. And sure enough, there he was—Mr. Owl—quietly sitting on a limb.

"See!" teased Johnny and Teddy. "We told you!"

Mr. Owl was surprised to see the young squirrels out so late.

"Whoa!" said Mr. Owl. "Do your parents know where you are?"

"Y-y-yes, of course," Johnny lied. "They said we could go to Mr. Smith's farm."

Ignoring the wise old owl, they quickly went on their way.

Finally they reached the farm. As the hungry squirrels jumped onto the fence, their mouths fell open.

"Wow!" Tammy yelled. "Look at those big acorns!"

They could not believe their eyes!

"What are we waiting for?" shouted Teddy.

In a flash they dove for the acorns.

The squirrels began munching.

"Mmm! Mmm!" Never had they tasted such delicious acorns. They laughed and shouted to each other, "These are the best acorns in the whole world!"

They ate, and ate, and ate...till their tummies could hold no more.

Now the young squirrels were so stuffed they could hardly move.

"I'm full," moaned Johnny.

"So am I," said Janie. "We'd better get back home before Dad and Mom find out we're gone."

They tumbled over the fence and began to waddle back to their homes.

The chubby squirrels did not realize it, but all their whooping and hollering had stirred someone from his sleep. Now, that *someone* was hungry! And he was creeping up on them.

As the slow-going squirrels reached the open field, out from the bushes sprang the big, bad wolf!

"W-w-wolf!" Janie yelled. "The big, bad wolf!"

Off they ran, as fast as their little legs could take them—which was not very fast since their tummies were so full.

The squirrels scattered in four directions. Since the wolf could not chase all of them, he ran after the closest one—Johnny!

Johnny ran as fast as he could—but tonight the wolf was faster. Johnny ran toward the nearest tree. The wolf drew closer and closer.

Johnny almost made it. But just as he reached the tree, the wolf jumped at Johnny with his big jaws open wide.

"O-u-c-h!" screamed Johnny.

Meanwhile, the others were so scared they raced home as fast as they could.

When Janie got home, she ran into the house crying, "Dad! Mom! The big, bad wolf!"

Dad jumped up. "What? What's going on?"

With tears in her eyes, Janie quickly told them what had happened.

"But where's Johnny?" asked Dad and Mom.

Janie shook her head. "I don't know. I saw the wolf chasing him, and then I heard him scream, 'Ouch!'"

Dad rushed to the window.

There was no wind, and the full moon lit up the night. Dad listened...and strained his eyes looking for Johnny.

Finally he turned around and with tears in his eyes said, "I don't hear him...or see him."

Mom hugged Janie as they cried.

"I'm going to search for him," said Dad.

Dad hurried, jumping from tree to tree. He met Mr. Owl, "Have you seen Johnny?"

"I heard a scream from over there," said Mr. Owl.

As Dad leaped to the top of a big oak tree, he heard someone crying.

"Could it be my Johnny?" Dad wondered.

With lightning speed he flew from branch to branch. Soon he came to a tree by the edge of the meadow.

Dad jumped onto a limb and spotted a scared little squirrel sitting on a branch—shaking and crying.

"Johnny!" shouted Dad.

Johnny ran to Dad and cried, "The wolf bit off my tail!"

Dad wrapped his arms around Johnny and held him tight. "I'm so glad you're alive!"

After making sure the wolf was gone, Dad took Johnny home.

Mom was staring out the window when Dad and Johnny came weaving through the trees.

"Janie!" Mom shouted. "They're here!"

Janie jumped up and down for joy.

When Dad and Johnny came to the door, Mom and Janie met them with big hugs and kisses.

While Mom bandaged his tail, Johnny told everyone how he was chased by the wolf.

Then he groaned, "Ohhh . . . ! If only I had run faster, this never would have happened."

"No, Johnny," said Dad. "If only you had listened to us, this never would have happened."

But Johnny *still* was not listening. He was mad at himself for not running faster.

As the days passed, Johnny's tail got better. However, with such a short tail he could not balance himself well. Now he was no longer the fastest at tree tag—he was the slowest.

Word of what happened spread throughout the forest until everyone knew about it.

Meanwhile, Johnny thought much about how he had lost his tail.

Mr. Wise Owl came to visit Johnny. "I'm sorry to hear what happened," he said.

"Well," mumbled Johnny, "that's *one time* I should have listened to my dad and mom."

"Johnny," answered the wise owl, "you should *always* listen to your dad and mom. They love you and they know what's best for you."

"But it doesn't always seem right," said Johnny.

"You need to trust them," explained Mr. Owl. "You will find it's *always* best to obey."

Johnny thought for a while. Suddenly his eyes lit up. "Now I understand! If I trust them, then it only makes sense to obey!"

Johnny's forest friends came to see him. He told them all about the big, bad wolf. When he was finished, he pointed to his short tail and said, "I was foolish for listening to others."

From then on Johnny listened to Dad and Mom. And in spite of his short tail, he became a very happy squirrel. And most of all, he was glad to learn: To disobey is wrong, even when you think *no one will ever know.*